Love Always Everywhere

For Luca and Ella with love
S. M.

First published in 2015
by Nosy Crow Ltd
The Crow's Nest, 10a Lant Street
London SE1 1QR
www.nosycrow.com

ISBN 978 0 85763 249 4 (HB)
ISBN 978 0 85763 250 0 (PB)

Nosy Crow and associated logos are trademarks and /or registered trademarks of Nosy Crow Ltd.

Text copyright © Nosy Crow 2015
Illustrations copyright © Sarah Massini 2015
The right of Sarah Massini to be identified as the illustrator of this work has been asserted.

A CIP catalogue record for this book is available from the British Library.

Printed in China
Papers used by Nosy Crow are made from wood grown in sustainable forests.

10 9 8 7 6 5 4 3 2 1 (HB)
10 9 8 7 6 5 4 3 2 1 (PB)

Love Always Everywhere

Sarah Massini

Love me

Love you

Love one

Love two

Love quiet

Love loud

Love shy

Love proud

Love lose

Love miss

Love smile

Love kiss

Love giggle

Love hug

Love tickle

Love snug

Love care

Love share

Love always . . .

. . . every

where.